THE GIRL I MET THAT SUMMER

ASHOK KUMAR

Contents

From the diary of Marco

Today was the first time my eyes cascaded on a countenance so smooth. I ascertained my eyes felt gently for the lineaments I was viewing were impeccable. I fear I may mar the unblemished face with my scrutinizing gaze...

CHAPTER ONE

WHO IS SAM?

"Marco! Marco! Wake up. We don't have much time I anticipated you to be on time...."

"Marco? Marco? Where..."

"I am ready."

"It is august you are ready so early? My intuition said so. Guess you genuinely appreciate visiting your friends and meeting Bella. How is she by the way?"

Magery said these in longing of eliciting an answer from Marco but had to get gratified with a simper.

Margery beamed as she left her son Marco's room saying these words. She went to Andrea's room but she was flabbergasted when she saw her tossing over her bed like a fish outside a pond.

"Andrea you're okay?"

"Not after eating those spicy shrimps Luca brought."

"My stomach's hurting a little... but some medicines will do."

"Fine, I'll grab water and medicine is in the drawer next to you just take them out."

Margery brought a glass and gave Andrea the tablets, when her pain was assuaged Margery said

"Get ready Andrea and yes one more thing quit calling your dad with his name people don't really appreciate that"

"Yes, I am aware but people already don't like me because I behave like a boy and don't roam in a camisole but in trousers. I ain't enough demure for them" said Andrea

“Andrea it is not like that sometime people just don’t show they love you but they do.” This time Margery’s voice was serene which Andrea had witnessed for the first time this morning. Andrea’s mom gave her a soft pat on the back and told her to get ready. It was a pleasant morning in the town of San Gimignano in Tuscany. The air wafting in the environment today had enigmatic wistfulness in it.

For the past few days weather has been searing but today it was slightly tempestuous. The drive
was about an hour. After Margery had her usual tête-à-tête with her kids and packed her luggage she sat down at the table where her husband was scrutinizing the newspaper.

With a cappuccino in her hands, she sat across him. They had almost the ideal relationship. Although their culture were not same but you know having trust and being loyal with a litte adjustment are the parts and parcels of any relation. For Margery Luca was a foible person at start but slowly things started to fall in place.She said “Did you pack your things? If you say something at the last minute this time, I won’t do it."

“Relax Tesoro, everything is done, and don’t fret no last-minute work this time. I assure you. But somethings vexing you?” asked Luca

“Marco’s sudden change has put me in a catch-22 situation, like a dilemma.” “What catch-22 situation?”

In a mystifying voice, Margery preceded to delineate her tribulations “He has become extremely faint and you know her class teacher Miss Mary couldn’t cease expounding on how silent he has become. She said his grades have not been great either. Last week our neighbor Mrs.James came over but Marco was benign with her whereas earlier he barely acknowledged someone how can you not mention how organized he has become now?"

“Wait wait wait... So you are nitpicking about his quiet demeanor!? That is the most ludicrous
thing I have ever heard this morning. This is even weirder than that guy who makes jokes like a nose can never be 12 inches long

because then it will be a foot!

Honey, you appear like that pedagogue to me who is worked up because his class is behaving well today. Shouldn't you be optimistic about our kid's growth? He was close to his grandmother, probably her demise..."

"No, the subject is this is such a precipitous change. I mean how is this even conceivable that he changed so much when we aren't even saying a thing to him? And if he had to change why didn't he transform earlier? We have been orienting him in manners for ages now. " said Margery agitated because of her husband's doltish talks.

The couple didn't notice amidst their profound conversation Marco had reached the table. Only when he comes too close to the table does his dad glance at him followed by his mother. Both parents anticipated him to mumble something but he didn't. His eyes were weary though he had slept, they were impoverished of sweet dreams. He perceived the whole conversation and at some point, even his parents knew that he knew everything but stayed silent. The contumacious silence was broken by the cacophony of Andrea's heels when she walked down the stairs wearing the most impeccable dress in her wardrobe perfect.

"Andrea, how did you manage to do it yourself?" said the parents as alexithymia takes over them

"I didn't do it mom Marco helped me, his impeccable style surprised even me, and you

know he did my curls today and..." But before Andrea could conclude expressing her surprise both parents looked at Marco in unison. Luca took the initiative this time and asked,

"Marco, you did this, who taught you?"

Marco replied, "Sam she is really good at these things."

These passing days as Marco has gained some enigmatic powers he was no longer the same Marco. He didn't play with his friends but chooses to spend his time at home, in his room. He has become strangely deferential, his grades degraded and the way he became aficionados in fashion was extremely perplexing for everyone. In school, he wasn't the clement child but akin to scholarly. Now he wasn't anymore. And Marco's mom was precise about his change but these changes weren't overnight. These things have been there for years but were imperceptible. His teachers perceived him as a boisterous student. His friend group had almost every student in the class. He barely was attentive but teachers brushed it off as he passed his classes with good grades and he wouldn't follow them either. But things took a wild turn when he met a girl named Sam one summer he went to his grandma's house.

But it was not until the penultimate summer Marco got to know who she genuinely was. Marco's mother Margery would consistently anticipate for Marco to become a mature person but his quietness was eating her from inside. Her intuition said there wasn't something right. These trepidations were haunting her and a constant feeling that she was under someone's vigil was always lingering. She had a constant feeling she was losing her son to someone but wasn't acquainted with that person or presence. She is ready to do what it takes to bring her son back before it is too late. She couldn't articulate her worries as everyone brushed them off and pointed to her that she was thinking too much but she can't help and wonder about only one person Sam. She witnessed her in dreams but has a feeling she is something more than just one dream. There is more to her than just one night.

This summer her only mission is to find Sam. She knows Sam is real!!!

From the diary of Marco

Like a Tulip she was benign, she made my heart beat fast but took my breath away. Is there any way I can convey to her my feelings for I feel my words are too decisive for her? So is my passion for her. Her simply being in that place with me is my sweetest souvenir but days without her are like lakes sans water. I desire to brush the hair falling over her temple but have trepidations that I might fortuitously sabotage the camaraderie...

CHAPTER TWO

MEETING WITH SAM

The first meeting of Sam and Marco was quite inimitable if you can call it so. Marco is 13 now but the first time he felt the presence of that enchanting face was when he was 11. Yes, they have a long story more likely an enigmatic love story.

You will apprehend as we continue reading more about them. The first time he saw her was on the day when he and his friends had blemished the tulips of an old age pensioner Mrs. Hilary. The scene appeared like annihilation has taken place. They were playing catch when the ball absconded and deposited in the garden with such force that it vehemently uprooted a few of the tulips. But Marco and Sam's rendezvous didn't take place till late that afternoon.

Marco and his friends did try to escape the scene surreptitiously but to their consternation, Hilary caught them redhanded and before they knew it they were standing in the scorching sun getting seared while Hilary herself stood under the shade of an awning listening to how barbarous they have hurt the innocent tulips. Leonardo, Andrew, Mattie, Andrea, Bella, and Marco were all acting ruefully.

Then Hillary said "Are you all feeling remorseful even a bit on what you all did? You all together look like a multitude of maniacs that are imminence to my poor tulips."

"Yes ma'am we are..." replied Andrea

"No you all are not repentant I can discern that on your face, don't you try to take me for a ride me, miss. Children these days have the audacity to contradict their elders." said Hilary

"Why is she being so clamorous? Does she ever going to stop?" whispered Marco

"We are inured to her umbrage and philippic denunciation.They were her late husband's treasured and I assume she will halt only when we are well roasted in the bask and be in the same place as her husband" whispered Mattie and though nobody was able to hold back their laughter they managed to conceal it by putting down their faces.

Just then Andrew said Ma'am we said we are sorry about your loss. Our ball accidentally crashed here and your flimsy Tulips got damaged but we didn't aspire to. Legitimately you are being such a disdainful lady that you are absolutely oblivion of what you are doing. The sun is so scorching that every soul saves for yours is burnt but you have kept us under this hot sun for the past 15 minutes striving to make us feel awful and make us appear felonious for something we did inadvertently while you are standing in shade. Our heads have become as searing as a frying pan and our extremities are impoverished of energy but still, you are not halting. I think it is you who needs to contemplate their fallacies and the next time you go to Church confess the sin you have committed by making us stand in the heat.

"You are again daydreaming Andrew, aren't you?" said Andrea with a sigh.

"No, I am not!" Andrew said embarrassed about the epiphany.

"Yes you were," said Leonardo

Hilary clutched firmly to her cherry and ash wood cane while she said "How unabashed you all are instead of standing tranquil you are talking and snickering. A selcouth demenour. Bella is the an unsullied soul but guess some notorious people influenced you. But don't agonize I know you are benignant but others save for Bella from today onwards you will come every evening to inoculate my garden... all of you. Now go" said Hilary

All of them were fuming with anger and as they vamoosed out of the garden and they sprinted home. Marco went to take a shower to melt down every dire and debauched incident that had happened. He hoped out of the shower and grabbed a blueberry yogurt wafer to munch on before he decided to grab the ice-cream. He came to the porch to grab to glance at the vehicle bearing his confections.

His mother aware of everything that had happened asked Marco "Where do you think you are going after ruining Mrs. Hilary's garden?"

Marco stumbled and in an erratic tone said "Mom, I swear it wasn't my fault, we were all playing but then Andrew missed the catch and the ball went flying straight to her garden. We tried delineating this to her but she wouldn't believe us. She was incongruous to all beseeches. And she even browbeat us into following her behests asking to take care of her flimsy flora. Mom I anticipate that if you will tell her to let us go she will surely do it. I am ascertained."

Marco's mother said in an austere tone "Son you and all your friends got themselves in dire straits and now you all can't dodge the bullet."

Marco was incredulous of what his mother just articulated and unequivocally he was livid but just nodded his head and got himself out of the serendipitous conversation. He was irked but perplexed he couldn't figure out on whom was he angry. Whether it was his friend who missed the catch and they ended up in that curmudgeonly lady's garden, or that lady who just couldn't hold her emotions for those impotent flowers and made them stand in the sun for god knows how long and boldly in her cantankerous behavior ordered them to take care of her garden or was it her mother who supports the decisions of that termagant lady. He came out of his house and a flash of all the events ran in front of his eyes. But his train of reflection was soon interrupted because of the confection. He had enough money to buy four ice cream cones. He just bought one. Today he was late. Usually by this time he would be taking a nap but due to Hilary's drama he was sitting in the porch with ice cream in his hands while he comteplated on his mother's words. Andrew and Bella arrived there too for getting their cones but Andrew went short on cash. He asked Bella but she had no chance to spare.

Marco had the money but didn't bother to care. Andrew asked and when he admitted to having possessed the needed sum Andrew started asking him and even after importuning Marco he didn't pay. Marco didn't pay for Andrew unless Bella said so.

"I won't do this again," said Marco

"Okay fine it is not like you paid for me you paid because Bella said so but thanks," said Andrew Bella blushed but converted the topic saying "So are we going to that lady's house this evening?

"No!" replied Andrew

"Are you kidding me I will never go to that wretched garden and to that old lady again she will make us do all the chores and will sit freely herself chanting Bible with a rosary" said Andrew

But Marco was quite Bella inquired to which Marco said "My mom thinks that we should go there and even if you guys won't come I will have to go. I don't think she will let go of me. I presume I will go. But that old lady was so benevolent with you Bella why should you do and get your hands dirty?"

Bella took Marco's hand and said that if he will go so will she, after all, she is a good friend right? Well, the reality is Bella appreciated Marco more than just a friend but never manifested her feelings though everyone witnessed this. And the way Marco was gazing into her brown eyes now it was conspicuous Marco too wanted to be with Bella but both never confessed. She would always find ways to be paired up with Marco during game, any gatherings or even if a simple walk and if she ever said Marco too would run to succor her. It was an apparent yet hidden relation.

Both knew but didn't knew the type of relation. Just as the friends were engaged in their usual chat they heard a girl talking to the ice cream seller.

"Uncle please see again..." said the girl

“No dear the money is not enough.” said the seller Andrew peeked and saw a beautiful brown haired girl of their age buying the mint chocolate chip like Bella but it seems like she didn’t have sufficient funds. Bella was about to speak when the girl turned around and requested the friends for help. Marco was extremely tentative but seeing her big dusky eyes filled with tears as she was pleading he paid. Bella was really liked that Marco paid for her with ease unlike Andrew.

“Thank you so much,” said the girl

“What is your name?” asked Bella

"Sam" said the girl

CHAPTER THREE

Marco and Bella

Marco before was an exuberant child someone whom you can call full of beans. He was whimsical and he spent the least time with books yet he passed. You can rarely spot his nose in the books he would hit the books only when there were terminals. He had a group of confidantes with whom he would always play when he went to his grandmother's house.

His and his friends' lives were teeming with escapade experiences. Leonardo, Mattie, Andrea (his sister), and Marco were not malovelent creatures it is just that parlous things kept happening to these ingenious people. Like one time when they were walking across the street, they were all happy until a mad Cane Corso started to run after them.

The day Marco met Andrew and Bella was also the same. Marco and his group were getting castigated for almost killing someone's dog with their batons and that is when Andrew and Bella saw them. They were siblings. The first time when Marco saw her he was stunned at her beauty. Her skin was unblemished; it looked like a snowflake, perfect yet enigmatic. Her face might have a smile but it was like the vacancies between the raindrops. Everyone knew they existed but were imperceptible. It felt like her eyes were the impeccable tribute to emeralds that could mesmerize anyone with just one look.

Her face and hair were the juxtapositions created by nature. The face had subtle movements with the equanimous expressions but the locks were dangling and dancing like the wind chimes creating gentle tintinnabulation during the tempestuous days. Her lips had slight emptiness between them as if they were saying something in a language transcendent to a common human. Those lips were the sumptuous imitation of Dahlia and it would be a crime if I compared her splendor to the moon for it had marks of imperfectness but she didn't.

If only Marco had the power he would have made people know that the real moon was in front of her and the moon they witness is just a shabby rock in space. It wasn't possible for a human to look this striking and have beauty this covetable. Marco was hankering for talking to Bella. But he was ambivalent about this idea. He thought to himself that he was the most scandalous child of the neighborhood and she was the quintessence of modesty. Why on earth would she talk to him? She had everything he can't. But just the conceptualization of not talking to her was killing Marco from within.

With a mixed feeling of apprehension and melancholy, he sat beside his grandmother. She was a lovely lady in her 80s but she was not like other old trout. She has been aging like a fine wine. Her husband passed away eleven years ago and Marco never saw his grandfather save for pictures that his grandmother kept preserved. His grandmother was alone but she busied herself with knitting, gardening, rearranging the house with her servants, and trying out new recipes. A feeling of euphoria rushed through Marco while talking to her. He went to her and at the rate of knots elucidates his entire feelings to her. The old lady gave a beatific smile and made her grandson sit by her side. She kept crosia work aside and looked at Marco.

She said to Marco "Dear what you experience and the anxiety you suffer because you are afraid whether you will see her again, whether you will meet her again, or if you will ever talk to her is called love. Remembering her when she is not there is love. Anxiety is because of your uncertainties. The sadness you have in the corner of your heart is because of the notion of losing her. It is your fear. You fear that she hates you for your notorious guise and she might decline you if you will converse with her. Am I right?" said grandmother Marco indulged in his grandmother's story and said nothing simply nodded.

"At your age love might be a decisive word and there are all possibilities of it being a simple infatuation but your feelings and worries say otherwise." said the grandmother.

She proceeded with a gentle smile serenely sitting on her lips, "When I first met your grandfather he was a wonted vendor..."

"And he was smitten by you?" interrupted Marco

"Son be a good listener. Just listen to grandma without any turmoil?" said Luca

"Her ballad is fascinating right?" said Luca and he too sat down beside Marco

"So where was I? Yes, he was a street vendor, and the first time I met him more likely our first encounter was in a local market. I learned from a couple of cronies that his name was Antonio. I didn't contemplate much and continued my excursions. I barely procured my parents' acquiescence to step out and I didn't want to dissipate my time digging for information about a vendor but fate had another plan for us. My parents were adamant about my security; they never conceded my demands of going out after sunset. They had their own tribulations since my dad was an influential businessman of that time there were indeed many hideous haints after me trying to impair me but I had just turned 18 at that time and like other teenagers, I barely cared about all the admonishments. So on my birthday amidst all the pompous parties and celebrations my friends and I sneaked and guess what? It wasn't the brightest idea."

"Did something happen to you nonna?" asked Marco

"Yes myriad things happened but that blunder turned out to be her saccharine tryst with your grandfather," said Luca with a smile

"Grandma your sweet voice and eloquence make you a raconteur," said Marco with a flimsy smile to which the lady smiled

"We all were going to the nearby park to enjoy the nighttime and to celebrate my birthday under the picturesque sky when a cluster of mafia assailed us. They vehemently tried taking all the possession but just then Antonio was passing by..." Marco's grandmother stopped saying as if she was re-living that night, that time, that moment when those pair of beautiful eyes of Antonio met hers.

"Grandma, are you envisaging the night?" said Marco tantalizing her

"No no...I mean yes I was a little but that night all I can reminisce about was how dauntlessly he saved us, he got bruises himself but he wasn't backing off. At last, many individuals gathered up and even the guards found us but I was soon unconscious because I couldn't take all that had just happened. My friends told me I fainted in the arms of Antonio when he approached me to hand my possessions" she was interrupted amidst her story by Luca.

"Your story sounds like a fairy tale!" said Luca "The more I hear the better it gets."

She simpered and enunciated "The next day your grandfather came to visit me to return the pendant that I had lost the previous night in that haphazard situation but all I can see was his face and only his face. We felt the ineffable spark and my sojourns to the market kept increasing...I rarely used to go near his stall but now it seems like a daily pattern to go there. I made up thousands of excuses and toiled to get my parents' permission, evading the guards and reaching the market. All of this just to have one glance at him.

Till one day I was indisposed and couldn't go to the market for a few days he came to my house. I was in the garden when I saw my guards having a feverish altercation with someone. On peeking, I saw it was Antonio I hastily summoned the guards to let him in and he appeared so anxious. His first question was where have you been? He said he had been staying late in the market for me every day but I didn't come."

She paused then said with a feeling of pleasure in her eyes "You know Marco at that we both knew what the other person meant. I didn't speak a word but my feelings were tacit. That minute and that moment we realized that the uneasy feeling we had while we didn't meet each other, the happiness and the coquettish smile that I had every time I saw him was love. When you think and miss someone who is not in front of you this is called love. Your grandfather didn't have high social status as us but that didn't bother me a bit and finally, my adamant parents who assumed Antonia was an acquisitive person needed to acknowledge our relationship. And your grandfather and I lived together for over 60 years until he broke his promise of always staying by my side..."

Grandma halted and there were pearls in her eyes filled with the satisfaction of having lived such a long time with his love but a slight hint of wanting to live more with him. To change the milieu Luca said, "Oh come on Marco it is already a quarter past 10 your mom will kill me if I let you stay awake any longer, go to your bed now."

"Mom you should rest do you want me to take you to your room?" said Luca

"No," said his mother

She didn't go to sleep until both Marco's parents begged her to sleep well and take care of her health. The next morning was the most awaited one. A tall boy, with bright eyes filled with sparks of a great future and with a classic front tousle stood there with fresh orchids in his hands like a little souvenir advancing towards someone words can't describe.

"Hi, these are for you," said the boy

"Oh! Th...thanks," said the girl having trouble articulating her feelings and surprise

"I am Marco what is your name?" said the boy

"Bella and these orchids are beautiful." Said the girl

"Glad you liked them," said, Marco Bella blushed and this is how their friendship began. They wanted to be lovers but didn't understand that they were never friends, the way they understood each other they were definitely not friends but let us leave their future in the hands of time and fate.

From the diary of Marco

She does 't appear to be of this world. Her smile, her aura her beauty is divine. I saw her for the first time. I didn't know what was that was binding us both but it felt like I have known her for a long time. But there is someone or something between us that is always trying to sabotage our relation. I fear that I might lose my love.

I don't know how long I can bear this pain that I am going through but at last I just want her to know that I love her and always will. There might be turmoil but I will love her. I am not dying because of this pain but because I am not able to tell her how much I love her.

CHAPTER FOUR

SAM'S PORTRAIT

Marco two days after the incident was strolling down the street with his friends in the summer. Marco, Andrea, Leonardo, Andrew, and Mattie were moseying. He didn't go to the garden and wasn't planning on doing it any time soon. He had been deluding his mother for the past two days saying he was toiling in the garden working among tulips, accompanied by soil and worms under Hilary's inspection, and instead just roamed with his companions. He assumed he succeed in hornswoggling her.

The sun was about to set. It felt like you blink and the sun is down. Just then Bella came and everyone knew that now Marco will abscond them and join her in going to their special place. Marco was an astrophile and he loved gazing at the stars in the night sky. From the day Bella coalesced with this group Marco would always take her to that place.

It was selcouth because he loved to do this alone and sometimes with his sister but now he and Bella would always gaze into the night sky together. For Bella stars weren't an orphic subject but being alone with Marco under the light of the twinkling stars was enough for her to join in this monotonous activity.

"Are you coming from somewhere?" said Marco Andrew interrupted their sweet conversation just like any brother would do and said "From market. She went to buy flowers."

"Flowers, for whom?" inquired Andrea with a devilish smirk and Bella knew she was again going to get teased and as she had anticipated precisely that happened.

“Is it for someone special? Marco right?” Leo said with a jest shining in his words. Friends never let any opportunity of poking Bella and Marco slip. Bella had been listening to these remarks for a long time still she would turn red on every comment. Well, after all, their love was still a new one and at this juvenile period, it can be arduous to camouflage the feelings of love and affection.

“Come on stop pestering her, she probably...” Marco proceeded to say something to save Bella from the red hot minute.

Just then she said “No they are right these are for you. I met Mrs. Margery yesterday at the market and while talking about flowers she said that you liked tulips so I brought them for you, hope you like them.”

Marco turned to look at his friends who were giggling as Marco turned red but then Leo’s face changed.

“Are you all thinking what I am thinking?” said Leo. Marco completely evaded Leo’s words.

“Bella, Tulips are pleasurable and I really appreciate your gift,” said Marco agitating.

"No Marco aren’t you apprehending this? Is Tulip really your favorite flower or do you like them?" asked Leo. Marco passed a tentative glance at Bella and said "Not exactly"

"You know this is a reminder from your mom to go and work on that old Hilary’s garden. She must have asked that old lady about our work" said Leo fearing he would have to step into that garden again

“She knows? So let us just acknowledge the fact that there is no escaping the scene right? We need to go into that garden and work in that soil while bearing Hilary’s constant philippic attacks” said Mattie

“Is there no one who can save us?” Andrea said with a sniveling face

“Who do you expect to save us; even our own parents have turned their backs...” Marco was saying when Bella spoke “I will help you”

Marco looked at her and everyone looked at Marco "I mean I will salvage you all by conversing with Mrs. Hilary and I am pretty ascertain she will relent the matter this time," said Bella

"Really you think this will work?" said Andrea with a spark of hope in her eyes

"I will try my best," said Bella with a comforting smile Bella was in a dither about the plan but now that she has given everyone a ray of hope she needs to gather all her courage and talk to Hilary about it.

The friends all walked timidly to the garden. The walk was a silent one everyone was tentative about the working plan and all were quiet. Andrew and Mattie were not even able to keep up their pace. So Leo held Mattie and Bella supported Andrew by holding his hands firmly from one hand and another one around the waist. There was an apparent rise in Andrew's speed after that but Marco couldn't bear like a second of it. And after a few minutes, Marco saw Bella was so close to Andrew that there was almost insubstantial space between them.

Marco said in an infuriated tone "Andrew stop being so frivolous you are practically clinging to Bella if you are not able to walk then come here I will take you to that old lady's house and put you in front of her and say that it was you who threw that ball." Bella, Mattie, Leo, and Andrew laughed.

"Why are you all laughing?" Marco said looking at them.

"Come on Marco stop being so green-eyed. Every soul present here knows that Andrew is Bella's sister," said Andrea

"Thank goodness Bella you are not holding my hand, I mean if he can castigate Andrew he would have literally killed me right now," said Mattie

The group teased each other till one of them said that they have reached. Just then Bella spoke "You all stay here I will go and talk to her"

"Are you sure you want to go to that old lady's house alone, she is really weird what if she scolds you?" said Mattie

"Yes I am... we are really worried for you," said Marco followed by all others

"I know she can be really philippic but I will be all right," said Bella

Bella rang the doorbell but to no avail. She hollered "Mrs. Hilary, Mrs. Hilary, Mrs...." Bella paused and her friends peeked

"What happened, Bella?" asked Andrea. Bella ushered everyone to come, and when they reached she showed them that the door was opened. "What the sam hill..."

Marco wanted to say but Bella intercepted him

"This place looks like a mess, it appears a burglary has taken place. Every single thing is toppled over. And do you see that..." Leo was saying something when he over and fell down

"Be careful you fool" said Andrea as she and Bella picked him up. Sun was almost set but there was still enough light to make out silhouettes of things. But Bella couldn't believe what she was viewing. It appeared to be a human hand and from what her intuition says the body is behind the couch.

"Everyone come here, do you see what I am seeing or my mind is playing tricks?" said Bella, her blood was running cold and there was a sudden numbness in her body

"Don't panic anyone if we see something strange we can call the cops?" said Andrew as he approched Bella

"Leave it, it is not like anyone cares!" said Mattie but as everyone neared they were all viewing the same thing. Their mind kept narrating to them that it was probably something else and in the darkness, things weren't clearly visible but this was clear. One could never make such a big mistake. Just then Mattie stepped back and his feet landed on the patch of something liquid and the entire group noticed it.

It was more than they can bear and everyone quickly came out and sprinted to Marco's home since it was the nearest. But just then Bella noticed something no one else did. But she wasn't in the state of saying anything. The first thing they did was go to Marco's house and delineate the entire story before Luca dialed the cops. They were all shocked and shaken at that appalling sight. Margery tried calming them.

“We went there to apologize for our behavior to Mrs. Hilary but there we saw someone brutally murdered Mrs. Hilary. . . Her house was all toppled over and ...” Bella paused and Marco held her hand but it was futile because Bella was frighted by her words. Was frightened by what she saw. Margery went to Luca and they called the cops. “Mrs. Margery I saw something in that house too...” but as soon as these words slipped from Bella’s mouth she went silent. And Margery shrugged it off thinking as Bella was still in shock.

CHAPTER FIVE

MARGERY'S INVESTIGATION

At the present things weren't alike anymore. Every scene has become chaotic. That famous friendship and en vogue love stories are somewhere missing. They were once here, the streets, the lamps, the parks, the benches, the stars, and this sky are the witness of those sweet dreams that were emblazoned once in the eyes of a young couple but not all scents from gardens have dried. The eyes that saw the sunset together, watched the sun handing its kingdom to the moon and slowly going down, the eyes that saw the sky as plain as a swathe of silk getting bedecked with myriad stars, and eyes that had billions of dreams building up within them are now just filled with tears.

It is an excruciating discomfort to watch the dreams get shattered like urns of glass. Every part of the city that witnessed those ballads now doesn't want to converse about it anymore because of the pain they procure from it and the emptiness they feel. The stars don't shine that bright, the sunset isn't that mesmerizing. An entire kingdom filled with happiness got drowned in a harsh ocean wave that spared no one. But now someone is there who has pledged to bring that time back. Bring that friendship, that relationship that loves back. And to get these back she needs to go back in time. But she is determined to find out what caused that wave to come and how it managed to destroy such a lovely city. She needs to know what occurred that night. Her last hope is Bella.

She proceeds to go to her destination.

"Bella are you home? Bella are you there?"

"Who is this? Ohh... Mrs. Margery, please come inside. Would you like to have something?" Bella was no longer that sweet and playful girl. She was now silent and rarely spoke; She was serene but this wasn't maturity but sheer sadness. Her parents are really worried about her but because of a function, they had to leave her.

"No dear thanks. Your parents aren't home, and your brother?" said Margery

"No, they went out for a nuptial. They will return within a few hours. Are you here to meet them?" said Bella

"You know Bella why I am here. You need to help me out. I have been to Andrea, Leo, and even Mattie's house, and before coming here I even asked Andrew but no one knows anything. They say that Sam was in Mrs. Hilary's house and you were the only one who was able to stay there but others fled away. They told me Sam had a guise like a ghost and probably she is one. Dear, she has been torturing Marco and I can no longer see his deteriorating health. Bella, I know that you are broken from the inside. The cold vibes that you have got from Marco have shattered your hopes and your dream and turned you from bloom to a dried flower. It must have hurt you a lot but I am with you, Bella. There is not a second that goes by when I don't think about you and Marco. Please tell me everything about that night."

Dear, I have felt your love. I have seen Marco's love for you. I have seen the dedication you both had for each other. I have seen the commitments but name the wind that blew your amicable world apart. Please Bella you are my last hope. Please..." Bella couldn't hold it any longer and she allowed herself to express her feelings through her eyes. Within a blink, her eyes were filled with tears brimming from her eyes through her cheeks drenching her dress in the pain she had kept hidden for so long.

"Marco's behavior hasn't hurt me, it has killed me. Marco has annihilated my love not once or twice but every time I tried to rejuvenate our love. Every time I remember seeing him with Sam I feel like my world has been torn apart again. Every time I remember Marco and the moments when he evaded me I couldn't help but think that whether he liked me at all or was this all an immature infatuation..." Bella was about to say more but just then Margery stopped her. "No dear, for god's sake don't enunciate such harsh words that Marco didn't love you. He did but now he doesn't recognize himself...When Marco speaks it is like he is no more under his control. Sometimes when Marco is better he writes in his diary where never forgets to mention you."

Bella's eyes widened at the revelation when Margery took out a paper from her purse. Bella in an instant recognized the writing as Marco's Marco's diary said "I don't apprehend what is happening to me. Bella, mom, dad is there anyone who can hear me? I have dreams that my grandmother wants me to stay away from someone but from whom? It is Sam. She is constantly with me. I can't focus on anything. Bella, I love you and you know I always will...Sam is rubbernecking me I just can't bear it..."

"He wrote this a few days before coming here. He wrote your name even before ours and if this doesn't make you believe that he loves you then I don't know what will" said, Margery

"I want to see Marco, Mrs. Margery," said Bella. Her voice had a concoction of fear, anticipation, and a hint of long-awaited love.

"It would be unavailing Bella! All he emits about is Sam. Sometimes he even pretermits his own name but not her" said Margery Bella once again broke down seeing how heartbroken Bella was Margery told her

"Now is not the right time to cry dear, you need to tell me what happened that day. Tell me who Sam is?" Bella composed herself and said "Not who but what"

"What?" asked Margery.

"Yes, Aunty Sam is not like you or me she has no corporal existence. She is an apparition" Margery's eyes widened as she heard Bella and she was more shocked at how Bella had kept such a whacking clandestine all to herself.

"You remember the time when we all found Mrs. Hilary dead in her home?" Bella said to which Margery nodded "That day everyone saw the corpse of Mrs. Hilary but there was something that I saw and others didn't and it was a mundane portrait with a face carved on it I will never forget." Bella paused as if trying to keep a tight rein on emotions and stopping herself from freaking out at her own words.

"Portrait, what portrait you saw Bella?" asked Margery

"Sam, it was Sam's but that had a message inscribed on it. It appeared like the note was written with nails like that of varmints. It had the message *I am not dead emblazoned on it*" said Bella

"It was named Samantha, and I was shocked at the resemblance of that portrait to Sam. Moreover as far as I discerned the notation was written with blood probably of Mrs. Milary's. And my trepidations were established that day when I witnessed her enter Mrs. Hilary's house after her demise. And what staggered me was that the house was sealed at that time. Sam would always find an excuse to be with us and take my place. Her intentions were malevolent, I remember once when we were playing she abruptly felt dizzy, and even though Andrea and I were near her she somehow managed to limp and take Marco's help. She would constantly try to make the connection with Marco and would always interrupt us if we were together. One day while I was coming with Andrew to meet Marco I witnessed her from a distance deliberately tripping and landing in Marco's arms. Everyone witnessed how Sam always tried to make the fact that Marco loved her tacit. One day Andrea, Leo, and Mattie inquired me whether I had ambiguity about Sam. I did but explained to others I didn't. For I didn't want to appear like a dubious person who suspected their own love though Sam was shady to me from the very beginning. Then the other day I saw her she was presenting orchids to Marco and he once told me that they were his favorite. He accepted them with the same smile as he did for me.

I was heartbroken and confronted him. Then he claimed Sam informed him that I gave her the flowers to give him. I didn't want to discover more so I let it go but I couldn't apprehend one thing about who informed her that orchids were Marco's favorite. Only I knew in the entire group about the flowers, others were oblivion about this matter. But following that Marco evaded Sam always and things went back to normal or at least I thought they did."

Bella stopped as if the past was still unacceptable to her.

"Please Bella," said Margery, and Bella nodded before continuing

"One night Andrea and Leo came running to me while I was walking in my garden and they said that Marco was taking Sam somewhere and my instant reply was what Marco told me that he was fatigued and he wouldn't even go for stargazing. They didn't tell me much; they looked anxious and tugged me to the scene and Andrew came along me. I never thought about what I was going to witness will leave me traumatized forever. There I saw that broke my heart and crushed my soul. My dreams were torn apart and every bit of me just said that this is not true but the truth was in front of my eyes. I saw Marco and Sam sitting under the night sky and gazing at the stars. Sam was at my spot and Marco was embracing Sam in his arms. I thought of asking for an explanation at that moment but I couldn't. I couldn't live in dispair hiding the truth and I demanded an explanation and he behaved as if he didn't even remember me. He said he could recognize me"

Bella broke down and Margery offered her water. But she continued without it.

"Everyone adviced me tp move on but I was not giving up that easily. So gathering up all my courage I gallantly went to Mrs. Hilary's house again with my friends from where it all commenced. My intuition said so I did it. If it wouldn't have been for Mrs. Hilary we would have waited for ice cream that afternoon and Sam would have never seen Marco and me and if I hadn't gone to apologize I would have not seen all the other things. So I need to get to the bottom of this. This time it was sunlight and indeed there was the same portait and the identical message. I though I had hallucinated in darkness the previous time but it was real. But as I traversed to serach more about her there I saw her sitting on the same couch behind which Mrs. Hilary's body wss found.

Then within a blink she stood up but when I got out of the shock I realized she wasn't standing but hovering, her hair was wafting even though there was no trace of wind. I was terrified to my core but still, I asked her who she was. But others were so spooked that some fainted and some were still as a statue. I couldn't ask anything else and she whispered to me that Marco was only her before disappearing into thin air.

Bella paused and then continued "I don't know if she was a malevolent spirit but all I know is she is with my Marco hurting him." Bella gagged as her words mingled with tears. She wasn't able to take it anymore.

"Stay firm Bella if not more me then for Marco," said Margery in an affirming tone. Bella nodded "I tried telling this to my parents but they presumed I was depressed and couldn't accept that Marco had moved on. So I buried this truth deep inside me. But Marco never moved on. His empty eyes say it all. He needs me he needs us but I don't know how?"

"I know," said Margery ushering Bella to come with her

CHAPTER SIX

WHO WAS SAM?

Margery took Bella with her to the church. The air was soothing still Bella was still in utter bewilderment as she was still not sure if Margery understood how perilous this situation was.

"May I ask you something?" said Bella not sure of her own words

"Sure," said Margery

"Sam isn't going to back off this easily. She has kept him possessed for so long. I am sorry but the condition is more serious than you discern" said Bella a part of her believing that Margery would be disenchanted.

"Bella I know this looks cliché like all the Hollywood movies but let us be honest we have no other place save for the church where we can get a solution to all our problems," said Margery, and Bella gave a noncommittal nod.

Bella was not suspicious of Church or its power but felt an eccentric feeling going to the church. The ambience was not as she recalled earlier probably because she hadn't visited there since things went downhill in her life. They proceeded and after reaching the church and praying they looked for the priest who was renowned in the town for his power to heal people. Rumors were he possessed ethereal powers with which he could do anything yet he chose to serve people and live a simple life. The priest indulged in reading some books and just then Margery greeted the priest and gradually narrated the entire story and delineated her problems.

Bella and Margery waited on tenterhooks to listen to the priest's reaction. After a minute of contemplating, the priest said "Take me to the place where you noticed her portrait." With Bella's help, they reached Mrs. Hilary's house and got the portrait.

The house was in the worst condition. The doorknob wouldn't budge but when the priest tried the doors flew open a malodorous smell engulfed them. Bella and Margery covered their nose but everything seemed impotent against the smell. The priest ordered Bella to take the portrait down. It was arduous to stay even a second longer but they knew they have to do it and the painting wasn't high so she accomplished the task. This was the first time Bella was this close to Sam, her eyes looked so bewitching, her lips were soft, and her skin was slightly pale. But her tiny face and her voluminous hair looked great together.

Bella perceived that she had been scrutinizing Sam's portrait for quite a few seconds now. Margery and the priest called her and she got back to her senses. It was as if Sam had subjugated her. Bella moved but as she turned around her heart skipped a beat and she bellowed at top of her lungs.

That second Bella and Margery uncovered their nose as if the smell didn't bother him anymore.

"You will never apprehend, right? I am aware that this old abominable lady loved you. So let me send you to the same place as hers" it was Sam in a guise that was even more ominous and intimidating than what Bella remembered from their previous meeting. She pointed towards another painting which was of Hilary

"I...I...I" Bella stammered to speak even a word and her weak body was quivering she almost stumbled over the small table kept at the side. Her face turned pale with fear and Sam's evil smile grew bigger as if she knew she succeeded in controlling Bella, just when she saw the priest gesturing for her to move forward.

"How dare you step into my parish and grasp that portrait?" Sam said in the most petrifying voice ever. Bella wasn't able to decamp but just then Margery shouted "Bella she can't impair you. Proceed Bella go outside with the painting."

Sam turned and lifted Margery in the air. She was dangling like a leaf from a tree and seeking the opportunity Bella made a run for outside but the doors were closed just as she tried to escape surreptitiously. She turned around to see Sam was standing right in front of her. Her hair wafted in the air even though there was no trace of wind in the room. It was arduous for the priest to control such an obstreperous spirit but he intonated spells to restrain Sam and within seconds Sam was gone.

"She is a vindictive spirit," said Margery when they came out of the house

"I am dubious of that," said the priest and Margery was looking at the priest in astonishment. All three of them left the house with the portrait.

"Father, may I ask something?" said Bella

"Yes my child"

"Do spirits have the power to take the soul of the person they like?" asked Bella

"Yes they do," said the father. He already knew what was agitating Bella.

"Then why Sam didn't take Marco? She tortures him and if she isn't taking him why doesn't she leaves him?" said Bella tears rolling down her cheeks

"Your love is pristine. Marco and your feelings are chaste and therefore Sam isn't able to take him. She ought to shatter the bond of love between you and him before she can take him away" said, father. Bella was crying but this time her tears bellowed true love. She was happy to know that Marco still loved her the way he did when he first saw her. Their next destination was Marco's grandmother's house. By the time they reached there, it was the time of sunset. Luca saw them and couldn't hold his curiosity.

But before him, Margery asked, "Where is Andrea?" "I sent her to Leonardo's house as you said and Marco is in his room" replied Luca. He inquired about the portrait and listened to the entire story with a shocking expression.

After which he said "Oh, Mio Dio!!! Is this true Margery? My Marco my son is he...?" inquired Luca; he was too shocked to even articulate his feelings. His feelings were in the appearance of words but still dangling in the air and couldn't be apprehended by anyone in the room save for Margery. The billowing curtains made a guise of a human and startled Bella.

"Yes Luca it is true Sam is not a human she is a presence a terrifying and unholy presence. She has been with Marco for a long time...She has been torturing our son, making his nights teeming with nightmares, making him have breakdowns, and slowly trying to kill him..." at this point, Margery couldn't articulate the inexplicable pain her son must have been dragooned to go through. Her eyes brimmed with tears like clouds filled with rain and when eyes could no longer carry the weight of the feelings they flowed forming a river that said millions of words and so did Bella's and Luca's.

The priest gave them an encouraging look and told them all "We don't have much time; we need to get to work as soon as possible else saving Marco will become more challenging. If she comes don't be afraid" everyone nodded in agreement and did what they were supposed to. Bella and Margery together went to obscure every single mirror in the house. There were three floors Margery took the ground floor, Bella went to the first floor and Luca went to the second floor. Bella still had a feeling lingering around her that she was under someone's vigil. Just as she was obscuring the last mirror in Marco's grandmother's room she felt a tap on her shoulders.

"HUH?" "Who is there?" said Bella in a trembling voice.

The door she left ajar was completely locked. She bolted to check the door but it wouldn't budge. She knew what or rather who was there behind her back but still she turned back to face the mirror she saw her

"You think this stupid covering of mirrors can stop me from ending your story?" said the voice that was enough to stop the heart from beating. Bella could actually feel how fast her heart was throbbing in her chest but she recalled what the priest had told her.

"You are no one just an apparition, Marco always loved me, and therefore you were never able to take him away. You can control his mind but I will always live in his heart and he will live in mine you can't..." Bella proceeded to say more but just then the mirror broke with an ear-piercing holler of Sam and shatters of mirror scratched Bella in the face and neck. But the door opened and Bella with blood tricking down her face came out of the room.

On the second floor, Luca too was trapped in the room and Margery slipped hurting her ankle. Luca wasn't harmed but got a slight enigmatic cut. Margery was appalled at the sight of Bella staggering and walking erratically. "Bella! What happened to you dear, did you encounter her?" asked Margery Bella nodding her head "She met me, while I was in grandmother's room but I didn't even flinch, I made it apparent that I loved Marco just like he loves me and he can never be hers."

Margery could see the power, passion, and love in eyes of Bella and gave her a warm hug before Luca came to join the trio.

"Are your legs paining?" Bella asked Margery

"No I felt like someone pushed me and I hurt my ankle due to the fall but I anticipate it is a minor injury," said Margery

"What? You broke your ankle and Bella who did this to you? And even I got locked in one of the rooms" asked Luca who couldn't apprehend what was happening in the house he grew up in.

"It was Sam. She is the one who locked, the one who had hurt Bella and compelled me into falling" said Margery

They were worried and together advanced to Marco's room. There were three other priests also present along with the main priest and Luca hastly covered all the mirrors in the room and had tied Marco's hands and legs to the bed.

Margery and Bella sat outside as Luca treated both and returned to Marco's room.

"We should start!" said one priest and the others agreed And they started enunciating prayers but to no avail. Not a single movement was there but just as one of the priests placed a cross on Marco's head, he made a blood-curling scream.

"She is here!!" said the priests Sam was inside Marco's body and with a smirk, she said in a voice that neither sounded like girl nor body, "You think that with your flimsy prayers you can terminate me from his body. He is mine forever...aaahhh" Sam clamored in agony as one of the priests bestrewed consecrated water over her and dents of burn were conspicuous. Enraged Sam made the bed with which Marco was tied pendent in the air and turned the bed upside down. "Leave us else I will make the bed fall and Marco will perish at once" saying this Sam began giggling rancorously.

"Aren't you besotted with him?" said one of the priests

"Don't engage me into your fanciful and ludicrous dialogues. Vamoose or else" Sam left the bed to fall but halted midway when priests were inclined to comply with her behest and made the bed upright again.

Margery was feeling better and hearing all the clamor and chaos Margery with Bella's assistance entered the room. Marco appeared emaciated and Bella couldn't stem herself from whimpering and emblazoning her love from her eyes. Sam glared at Bella but shrieked in discomfort. Priests were able to yank her out from Marco's body. Bella scampered to untie Marco but Luca ceased her, making her almost lurch.

"Now isn't the best time Bella" but Bella didn't pay heed to any of the admonishments; she hastily untied all the knots and embraced Marco who was reclined unconscious in bed. A long-awaited cwtch, an emblem of immaculate love. Bella couldn't cease sobbing as she scrutinized the lineaments of the person for whom she is alive even after so myriad tribulations. Sam was frowning at how delighted Bella looked and at once Sam faded into delicate air.

"Stay away from him..." hollered the priests but before she could apprehend the words of the priests, Sam had already penetrated into Marco's body and inserted a sharp shard of glass into Bella. At once Bella's vision became opaque as Sam smiled viciously "Now he belongs to me." The priest and Marco's parents were appalled but with the might of prayers, they again seized Sam. Bella had lost a lot of blood and Luca scurried her to the hospital.

"Who are you and why are you hurting these people?" said the priest.

Sam was infuriated and gave them stern looks till one of the, again squirted the consecrated water she blurted "I am Samantha and that old woman whom I murdered that Hilary was my grandmother. Her son, Jack had wedded my mother Shuli when he came to our townlet once regarding work. There he first witnessed my mom's beauty and instantly felt enticed and infatuated by her. My mom was naive and though everyone precautioned my mother regarding wedlock as Jack will leave for the metropolis soon and there isn't any guarantee if he will return but my mother paid no heed to the admonishments and married him unaware of the repercussions. She was head over heels in love with him and Jack also pretended to. They kept their marriage surreptitious and just after a year of their marriage mom became acquainted that she was expecting me but Jack didn't visit her then. I was only four years when I had to witness my mom dying gradually and painfully from cancer. She promised me that she will soon recover from this notorious illness and would play with me but she broke her promise. She was brave and fought till her last breath but cancer was more decisive than she was and I lost her at 4. You all will never understand the pain of losing your mother when you are just four. One month after her death Jack returned and I was able to identify him because of the images my mom showed. How can I forget the man because of whom now I can never listen to my mom humming."

The room was absolutely hushed. The panorama was bewildering and eccentric. Every soul was feeling sympathetic for someone not even alive. For a second everyone forgot the pain Sam had given to Marco and Bella and for the first time people saw that innocent, innocuous, and tortured soul behind that revengeful face. She looked delicate more than intimidating.

She was not bad just broken. "I didn't desire to go with him to the city and I recounted to him I despised him but he would cry his eye out in front of me so I have his chance but didn't go to the city. He pretended to be so amicable and candor in front of me and also individuals in my village ridiculed me with the name orphan so when I was nine I chose to live with him in the city which turned out to be my worst mistake. My grandmother never appreciated me but for a few days, my father was incredibly endearing and benevolent. He would shower me with presents, even made a portrait of mine and many more things but then in the appellation of business trips dad would be out for days weeks, or even months, and during his death, Hilary would treat me worse than a housemaid she would make me toil all day, all night and I lived like a waif in my own home. One day dad returned from his usual trip and I was thrilled to see him. I rushed out to see him only to encounter a scene that broke my heart into million pieces.

Dying wouldn't have hurt as much as looking at them did. He wasn't alone, with him was a lady. He remarried. He killed my mother and made me an orphan at such a young age, never tended to me and now he got himself a young wife and that was the last day I saw him after that he didn't return. Hilary would scold me and even beat me if I did something wrong. No one in my entire life was nice to me in my entire life save for Marco"

Sam paused and glanced at Marco but not her typical ominous gaze rather than a benevolent gaze emitting from an eleven year old and everyone felt extremely apologetic for such a young soul had to go through so much. "On the day of my eleventh birthday, I pilfered a few coins and went to devour ice cream and there I met Marco, Bella, and their friends. I was short on money and Marco aided me"

CHAPTER SEVEN

FORBIDDEN LOVE BLOOMS

Margery with a serene voice and brimming eyes said " You are not the only one Sam who lost her mother. I never saw my mother nor my father from as long as I can remember. And Bella told Marco to help you but you tried to kill Bella?"

"No" shouted Sam

"Yes that is the truth whether you like it or not," said Margery Sam was again being obstreprenuous when priests controlled her and asked her to further delineate her story.

"Marco was the first person to support me but I couldn't meet him after that alive. That day when I arrived home Hilary was waiting for me and she was so incensed that day because of the Tulips that got eradicated that she embark to punch me and then she propelled me so forcefully that I slammed my head on the mantel of the fireplace and died. That night she buried me in her backyard, my dreams, my anticipations of getting love,my hopes about a better future, and feelings of seeing Marco again were buried. But I still couldn't get free I rambled as an apparition but Hilary protected herself with a Bible and some water always in her hand but after two whole days I got a chance to slay her and I even detached the hand from which she had pushed me and I want Marco now I desire to be with him" Sam said with a beatific smile

"Sam I know you had a very formidable life with foul people around you. We all feel remoursful for you had to lead such an unsettling life. You didn't deserve that you were a young and ingenuous soul. Everyone deserves to lead a festive childhood with their mom but your right was nabbed by this vicious society. You are just like my child but you can't impair others, Sam. Marco loves Bella, not you..." said, Margery.

But Sam shouted "He loves me he is mine. And whether you feel melacholy or not I will get procure what I desire. Your saddness won't bring my mother back and neither will it bring my life back"

The priest enunciated "What happened with you was not your fault but Marco loves Bella and she loves him. You are innocent doen't be a villian" Sam was getting weak and said in a feeble voice that Marco was her but the priests collared her in a vessel before she could get her power again.

One of the priests said "It was appalling and at last, she was a juvenile soul. She deserves an honorable burial. I desire she gets peace" Marco woke up and he appeared weak and famished. His mother was so astonished that she couldn't acknowledge her vision's accuracy. She embraced him with a close-knit hug and for the first time in years, Marco embraced her back.

She heaped him with canoodles. Marco had difficulty enunciating and he stuttered "Ma Bella, Dad where...?" "Everyone is salubrious they are fine they are fine" and then Margery broke down. "Sam will be in peace when we bury this vessel with her body, said the main priest "Yes," said Margery "I anticipate accomplishing that tomorrow, " said the priest The priests vamoosed from the property and Margery was isolated with her son.

Marco said he wanted to use the lavatory and she helped him and escorted him there. A few minutes flew by but Marco didn't come out. Margery got a little anxious; she didn't want anything to eventuate after all Marco had to go through. She hears a feeble cry and immediately barged inside. There she saw Marco standing precariously while taking support from the sink looking into the mirror and tears sprinted down his face. With brimming eyes, he glanced at his mother.

"What is the wrong son?" Margery rushed to wipe his tears when Marco said "Mom where is Bella? I know Sam injured her, right? Where is she I need to see her?" Before Margery could reply her phone rang it was from Luca. Margery was afraid to receive the phone in front of Marco as she knew Luca was about to say about Bella But she received it because she too was worried about Bella

"Margery?" asked Luca

"Yea," said Margery

"How is Marco?" inquired Luca

"He is all right. The priests were victorious and with god's grace, our son is standing all right in front of my eyes... How is Bella?" Margery was stunned by how these words tumbled from her mouth in presence of Marco. "Margery, can you move away from Marco?" whispered Luca through the phone Margery darted at Marco he signed her to stay.

"Thank god Marco is all right but doctors say Bella has lost a lot of blood. I am quite anxious regarding her health. Her parents were blasting my phone with calls and asking me where she is. I said that she got a little indisposed and therefore we brought her to the doctor and suggested them not to fret but I don't know how will we tell them the reality. I can't even envision what will happen to them if they know their daughter is in the emergency room" Luca abruptly ended the call as the tears mingled with his words were making it hard for him to speak. But Margery needs to handle Marco who just now woke up from a deep sleep and wasn't ready for this.

"Mom how did this happen?" said Marco with a face that made his mother feel devastated. "Nothing son she was just not able to hold the pain any longer..." Margery was silent and Marco's eyes were again brimming

"Sam did this? why?" asked Marco

"It wasn't her fault. She was nice but not loved. So she tried to stay with that one soul who supported her" said, Margery Sam recalled the day when he helped her.

"Where is Bella, mom?"

"Come with me," said Margery

They arrived at the hospital and were standing in incredulity when they caught a glimpse of Bella's parents over there along with Andrea, Andrew, Leo, and Mattie. Luca was sitting on the bench and when he saw them he stood up and explained that Bella's parents found out about the hospital and reached there. They would stop inquiring. All the friends gave Marco a friendly hug and it appeared like those precious days were back. All mischievous people were back again.

Margery said with teary eyes and a smile "All notorious people are back again but one person is missing" her smile fainted. Bella's parents stated to Margery

"Bella got a blood donor and now she is all right. We were fretting for our blood group didn't match hers but all thanks to the donor she is safe." Margery smiled and a look of relief was conspicuous on her face.

Marco who has been listening to the entire conversation said "Can I meet the donor who saved my Bella's life?"

"Sure," said Bella's mom. They went to the nurse who was supervising Bella. Marco was able to procure a glance of Bella after so long without being under someone's influence. She looked calm and sumptuous just the way he first saw her. The frivolous marks were not able to mar her impeccable face. Marco gently brushed her hair and gave her a gentle smooch on her hand. He was thankful that Bella is safe and ought to meet and thank the donor.

He turned around and said, "Where is the donor nurse?"

"Sorry you can't meet her she vacated a few minutes ago, but she left a note for a person named Marco. Who is Marco here?" said the nurse

Everyone exchanged a perplexed glance before Marco said "I am" The nurse handed the note. Marco read the note. While deciphering the words that were inscribed on the paper with ink he fell down to his knees with tears rushing down his cheeks. His friends supported him and Margery read out the piece of paper.

She loves you more than me and you too love her so I will leave you two but don 't think I lost, I just didn 't win this time. - Samantha

"Are you sure the person who donated blood was this girl? How did she look?" asked Luca

"Yes she was the donor, she had voluminous brown hair, brown eyes and she was definitely terribly young," the nurse said

"Has she returned again?" Marco said trembling before he quickly went to Bella and grabbed her hand firmly. He touched her to be ascertained that she is real and that she is still his. He wanted to make sure he can be with her now and forever.

"She has left for good. An innocent soul with a broken heart" said Margery

The following day Sam was given the decent burial she deserved. She went inside and the soil covered her as a blanket promised to give her a sleep teeming with sweet dreams. She departed not as any spirit but as an innocent soul who was seeking the love she didn't get while she was alive. The vile was with her when she went underground. Everyone was shaken by the sight, for the age that was supposed to be spent playing in euphoria on earth was now getting concealed by the earth. Within a few days Bella recuperated completely and the day she came home her friends and Marco's parents were waiting for her. Bella with a cursory gaze scanned the room but couldn't find him.

"Are you searching for someone sweetheart? Everyone is here" said Bella's mother

"Hmmm... seems like your sweetheart is searching for hers," said Andrea with a juvenile smile on her face.

"Who?" asked Andrew

"Come on man you can't understand a simple thing, don't you know your sister is searching for M..." just as Leo was about to expound about the matter Bella said, "Why he is not here aunty?" Margery said nothing and handed her a paper.

"The place where we first met"

Bella instantly recognized the handwriting and the hands who wrote this. She rushed to the field where she had first met him.

Friends also ran to the scene. There Bella saw that same tall boy, with bright eyes filled with yearnings, with classic front tousle standing there with fresh tulips in his hands like a little souvenir and advancing towards her. Bella came closer and Marco embraced her into a warm and long-awaited cwtch.

This time there wasn't any presence to tangle the moment. If a perfect moment ever existed it would have been jealous of this moment because it is more than just perfect. That eminent friendship and en vogue love stories that were somewhere lost and mingled are again in the air wafting through those streets, petrichor and flowers. Flowers were bestowed with scents that can never dwindle. The notorious and perfection were together again. They deserved this moment. Through ups and downs, their love survived and bloomed once again. Their meeting looked extremely dreamy. May God bless them and they stay together perpetually. There was emotion, love, and purity earned by loving each other in unfavorable situations.

"I am yours forever," said Marco, and Bella nodded with brimming eyes.

"I love you," said Bella

And as for Sam hope she gets the peace she deserved. She may not had the best life but she was the best. She didn't needed love anymore, she has made herself the defination of love and sacrifice. She was a survivor a beautiful innocent soul.

"I never realized Bella loved him this much," said Leo

"Guess it wasn't an ordinary infatuation. Their dedication and love brought them together" said Andrea getting slightly teary for her brother on getting such a reliable and lovely partner.

"Wish they stay forever like this"

"Yes," said Andrea

"What happened?" asked other friends

"What? You all said it" said, Andrea

"No, none of us said a word," said the friends

"What! Then who...?" Andrea's eyes widened at the epiphany She was here although innocuous but this is her land and she is always welcomed

From the diary of Marco

She wasn't bad just broken... My mom said and she was right. Sometimes sinister situations bring out our worst side. Sam was one of them. She went through circumstances one could 't even concoct at her age. She defied just like her mother and she prevailed. If I ever had to envisage her she would have an appearance of an angel and a sword in her hands. She was a warrior a valiant one...

9 798887 833996

Printed by Libri Plureos GmbH in Hamburg,
Germany